World of Reading

MARVEL

BLACK PANTHER

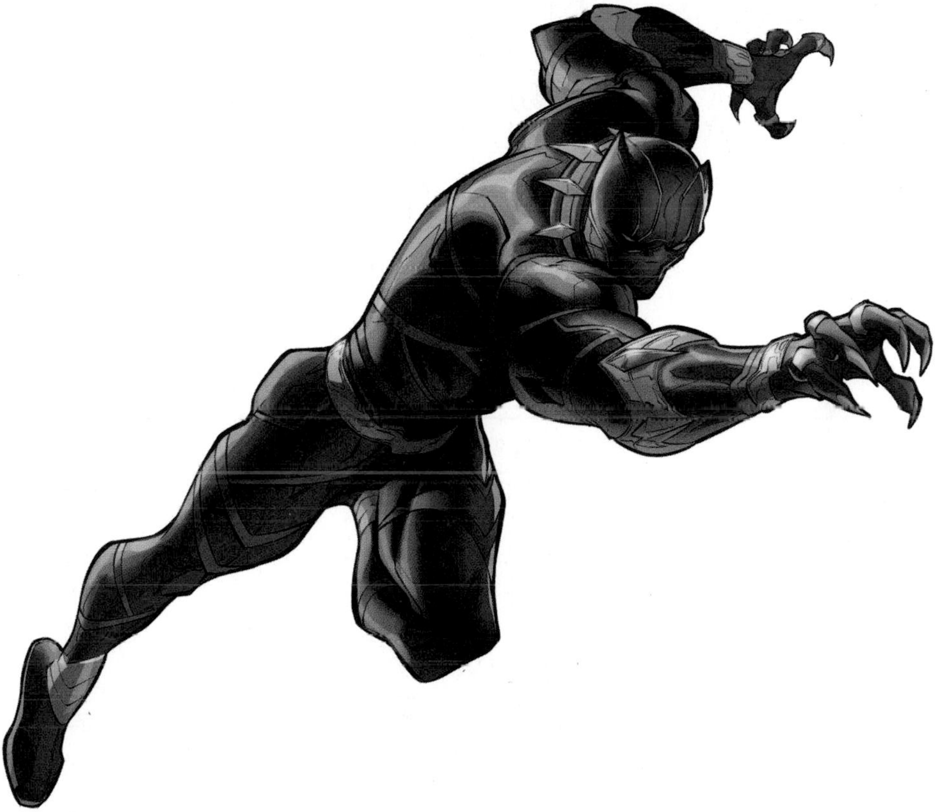

THIS IS BLACK PANTHER

Adapted by Alexandra West
Illustrated by Simone Boufantino, Davide Mastrolondardo, and Fabio Paciulli
Based on the Marvel comic book series *Black Panther*

MARVEL
Los Angeles
New York

MarvelHQ.com
© 2018 MARVEL

For information address Marvel Press, 125 West End Avenue, New York, New York 10023.

ISBN 978-1-368-00853-2
FAC-029261-17335
Printed in the United States of America
First Edition, January 2018
1 3 5 7 9 10 8 6 4 2

This is Black Panther.

Long ago, Bashenga was
the first Black Panther.

Black Panther is a
very important role.

Black Panther wears a suit.
He has super abilities.
He protects Wakanda.

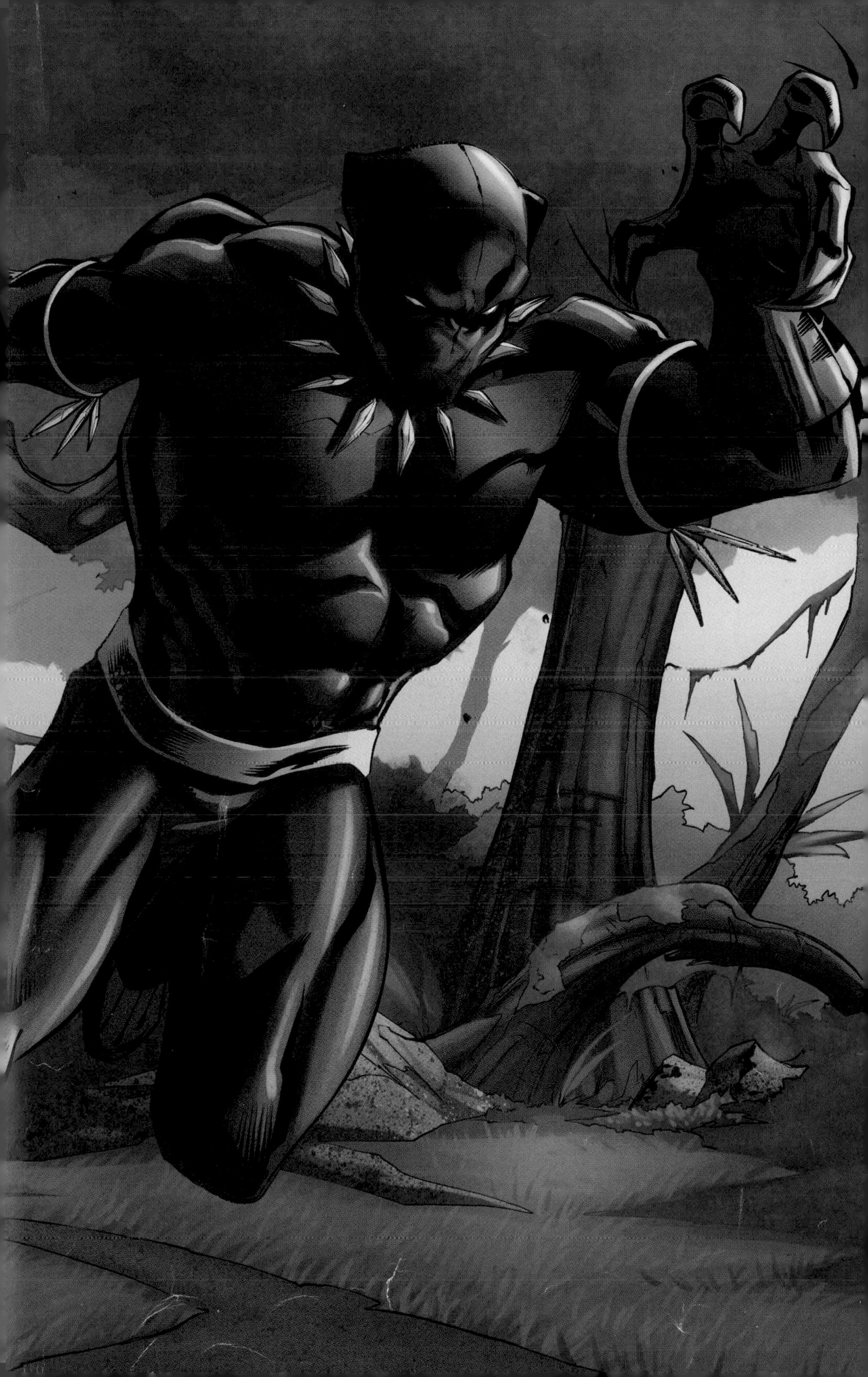

Wakanda is a country.

It is in Africa.

It has many resources.

T'Chaka is the Black Panther.
He has a family.
Ramonda is his wife.
T'Challa is his son.

T'Challa grows up.
He works hard.
T'Challa wants to be
just like his father.

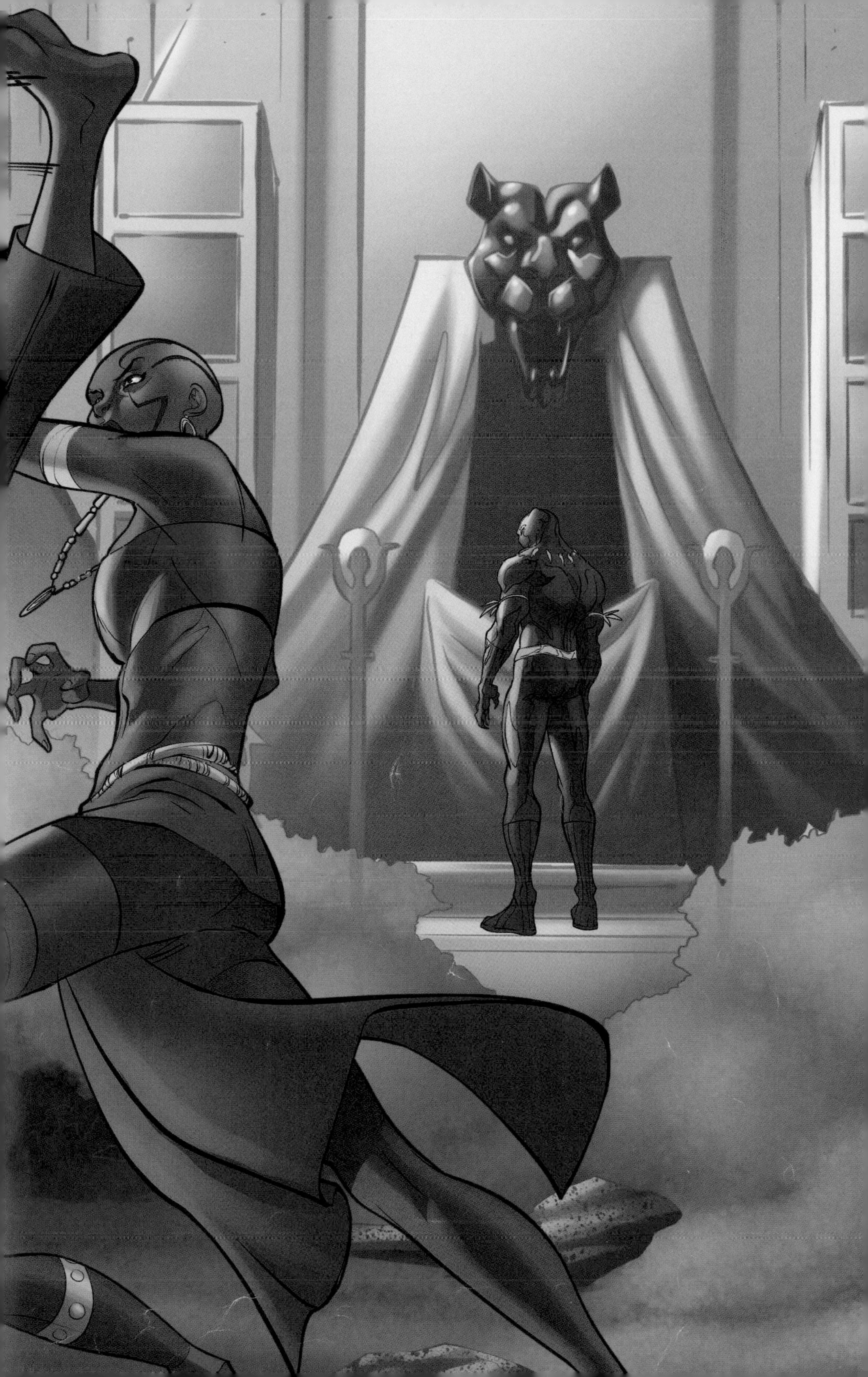

One day, a villain
steals from Wakanda.
His name is Klaw.

Klaw gets away.

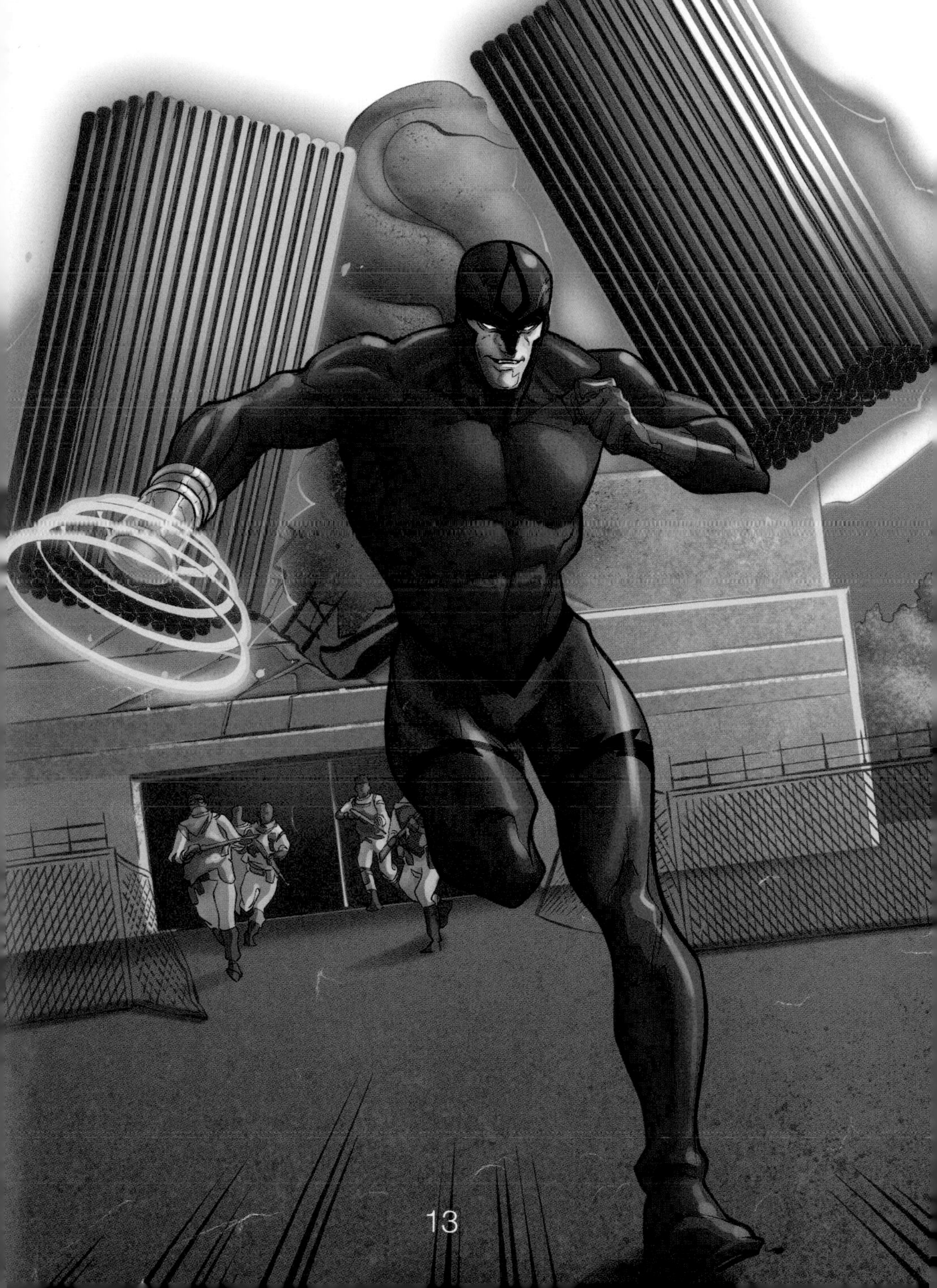

Black Panther tracks Klaw.
He catches the villain.
T'Challa follows.

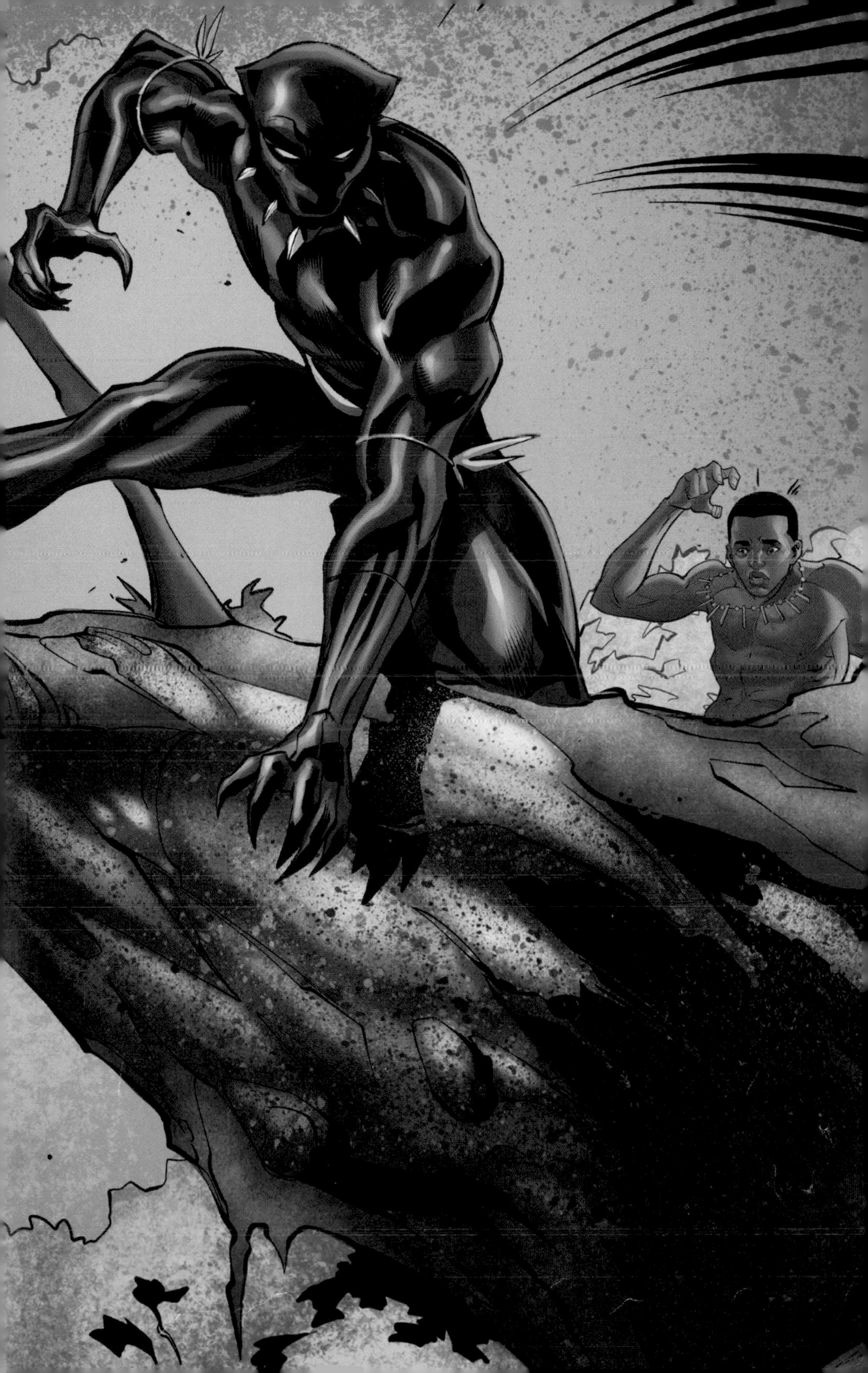

Klaw attacks Black Panther.
T'Challa shields himself.
But Black Panther is hurt!

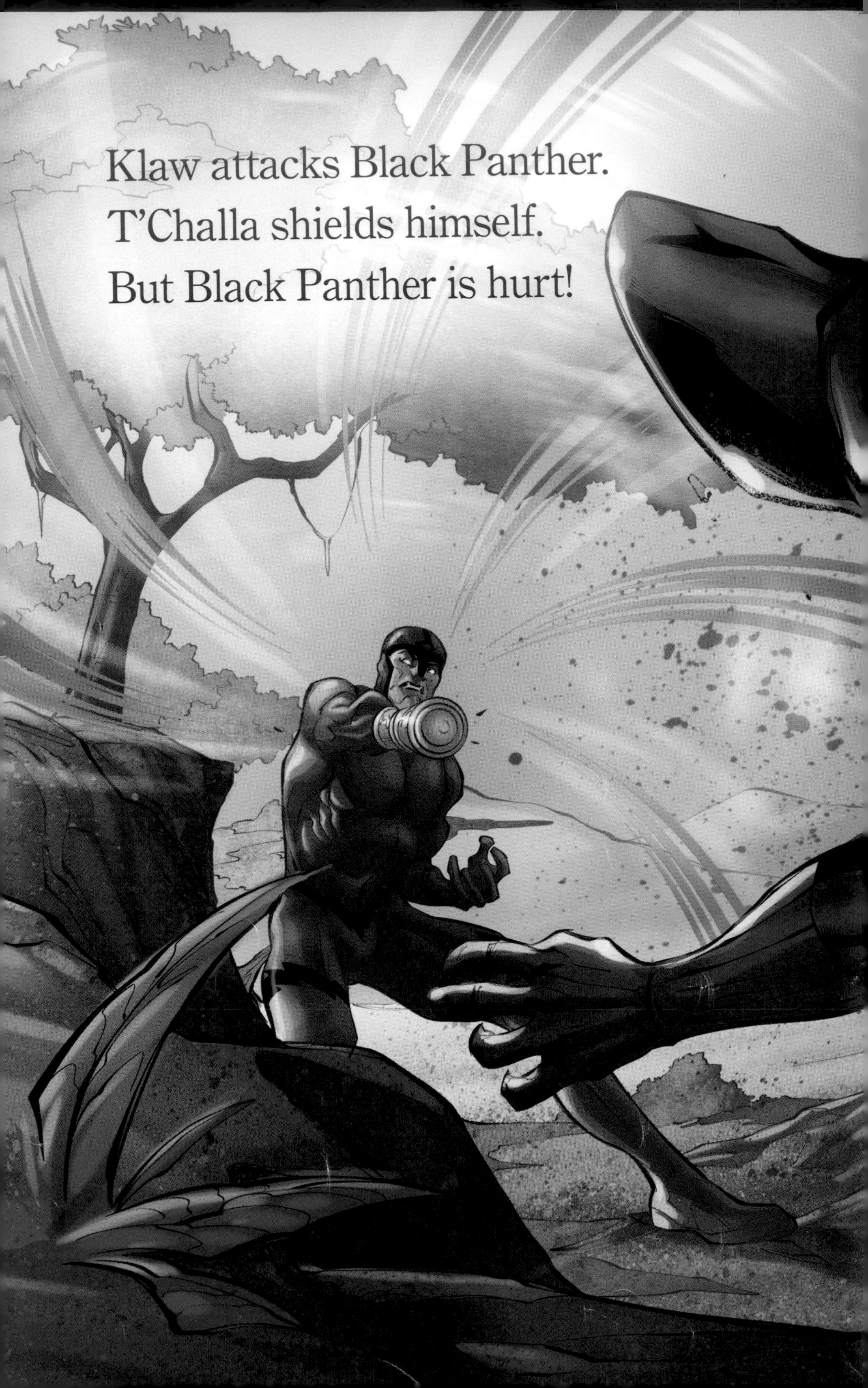

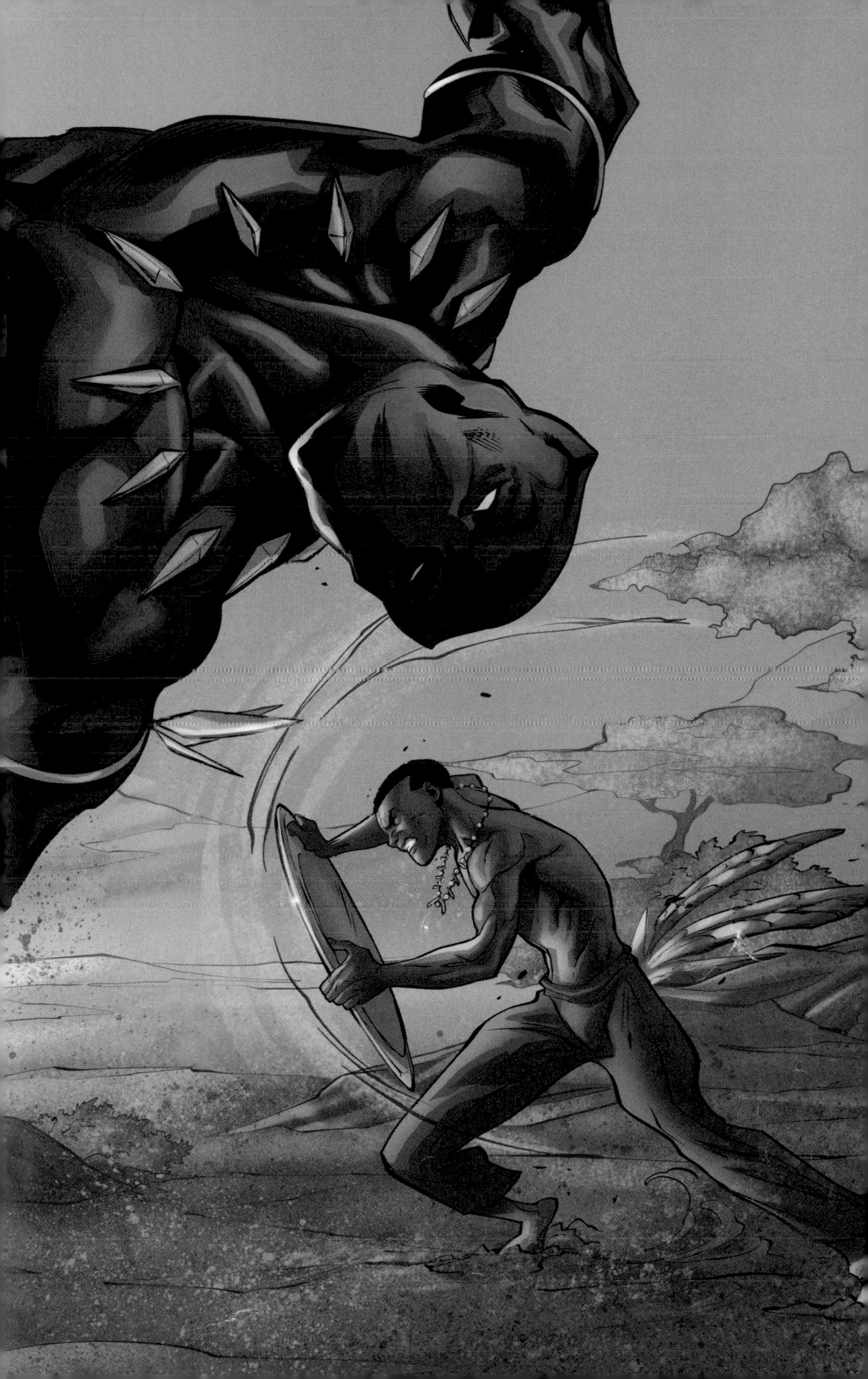

T'Challa tries
to fight Klaw.

Klaw escapes.
T'Challa holds his father.
T'Challa is very sad.

T'Challa will avenge his father.
He will become Black Panther.

T'Challa puts on his father's suit.
He needs to find Klaw.

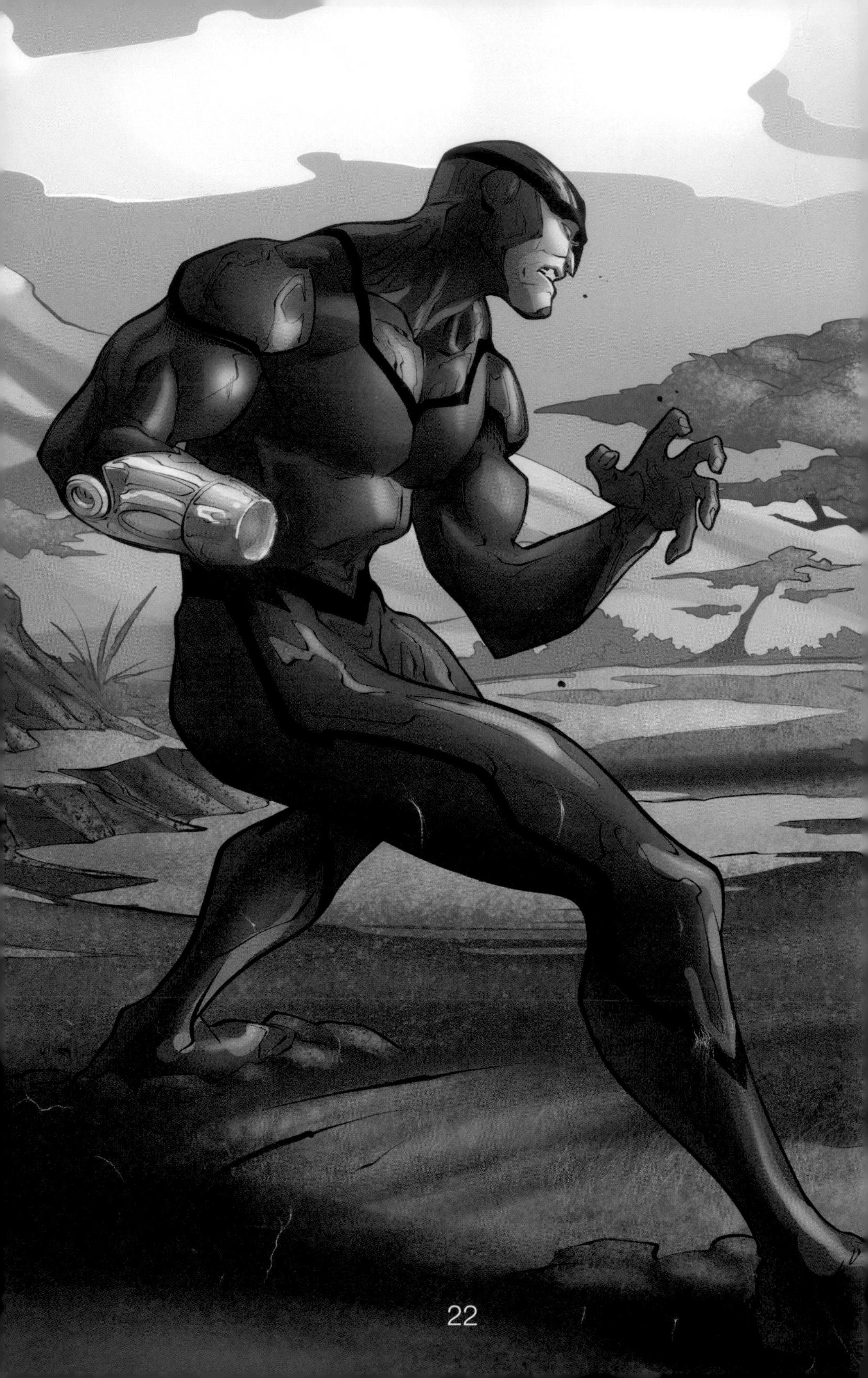

T'Challa finds Klaw.
They are both ready to fight!

Klaw is strong.
He knocks T'Challa
to the ground.

T'Challa is stronger.
He kicks Klaw.
Klaw flies through the air.

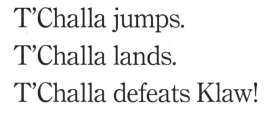

T'Challa jumps.

T'Challa lands.

T'Challa defeats Klaw!

T'Challa returns to Wakanda.
He kneels before his mother.
She crowns him.

T'Challa is crowned
the new Black Panther.
Everyone cheers!

Like his father, Black Panther
will protect Wakanda.
But he must also protect the world.

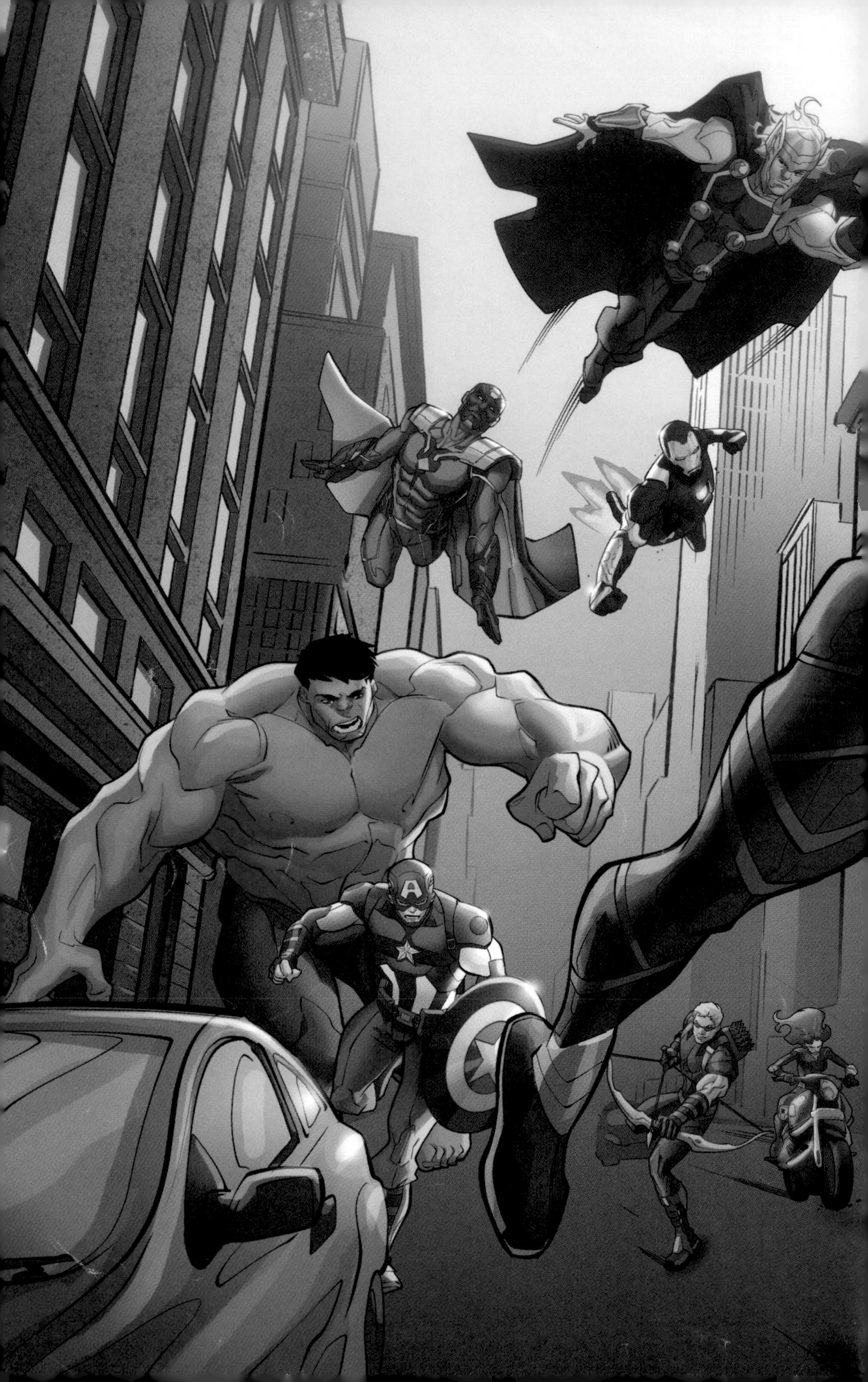

Black Panther becomes a Super Hero.
He joins the Avengers!

T'Challa is Black Panther!